D1373206

WITCHCRAFT

The Kingdom

The Palace

Burth

Mermaid's Cove

Crestwood

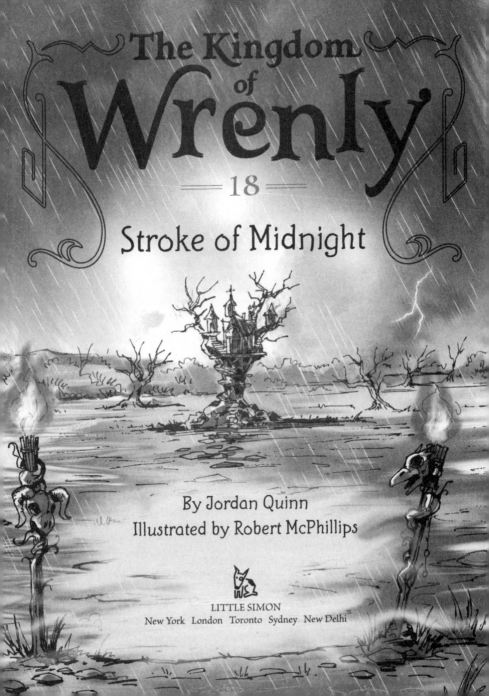

The Kingdom of Wrenly

18

Stroke of Midnight

By Jordan Quinn

Illustrated by Robert McPhillips

LITTLE SIMON

New York London Toronto Sydney New Delhi

This book is a work of fiction. Any references to historical events, real people, or real places are used fictitiously. Other names, characters, places, and events are products of the author's imagination, and any resemblance to actual events or places or persons, living or dead, is entirely coincidental.

LITTLE SIMON

An imprint of Simon & Schuster Children's Publishing Division
1230 Avenue of the Americas, New York, New York 10020
First Little Simon paperback edition September 2022
Copyright © 2022 by Simon & Schuster, Inc.
Also available in a Little Simon hardcover edition.
All rights reserved, including the right of reproduction in whole or in part in any form.
LITTLE SIMON is a registered trademark of Simon & Schuster, Inc., and associated colophon is a trademark of Simon & Schuster, Inc.
For information about special discounts for bulk purchases, please contact Simon & Schuster Special Sales at 1-866-506-1949 or business@simonandschuster.com.
The Simon & Schuster Speakers Bureau can bring authors to your live event. For more information or to book an event contact the Simon & Schuster Speakers Bureau at 1-866-248-3049 or visit our website at www.simonspeakers.com.
Manufactured in the United States of America 0822 LAK
2 4 6 8 10 9 7 5 3 1
Library of Congress Cataloging-in-Publication Data
Names: Quinn, Jordan, author. | McPhillips, Robert, 1971– illustrator.
Title: Stroke of midnight / by Jordan Quinn ; illustrated by Robert McPhillips.
Description: First Little Simon edition. | New York : Little Simon, 2022. |
Series: The Kingdom of Wrenly | Audience: Ages 5–9. | Summary: After a witch-in-training accidentally makes Prince Lucas and Lady Clara switch lives, the three kids must find a way to change Prince Lucas and Lady Clara back before the stroke of midnight.
Identifiers: LCCN 2021054950 (print) | LCCN 2021054951 (ebook) | ISBN 9781665919289 (paperback) | ISBN 9781665919296 (hardcover) | ISBN 9781665919302 (ebook) | Subjects: CYAC: Body swapping—Fiction. | Magic—Fiction. | Princes—Fiction. | Witches—Fiction. | LCGFT: Novels. | Classification: LCC PZ7.Q31945 St 2022 (print) | LCC PZ7.Q31945 (ebook) | DDC [Fic]—dc23
LC record available at https://lccn.loc.gov/2021054950
LC ebook record available at https://lccn.loc.gov/2021054951

CONTENTS

Chapter 1: Weird Weather   1

Chapter 2: Knock! Knock! Who's There? 15

Chapter 3: Head Games   27

Chapter 4: *The Book of Counterspells*   37

Chapter 5: *Switchity! Swappity!*   51

Chapter 6: Ravenna the Witch   63

Chapter 7: See You Later, Alligator!   77

Chapter 8: The Great Oak Comes Alive   89

Chapter 9: The Magic Ingredient   99

Chapter 10: Bubbles and More Troubles 109

CHAPTER 1

Weird Weather

Prince Lucas tied his horse, Ivan, to the hitching post in front of Wrenly's town bakery, The Daily Bread. The bakery was owned by his best friend Clara's family. Lucas jumped out of the way as Ivan shook the rain off his mane. It had been raining for days, and there was no sign of it stopping.

"Be right back," Lucas reassured his horse.

Lucas then walked up the stone steps and into the bakery. The bell on the door jingled behind him. He let down his hood and breathed in deeply. *Mmm, fresh-baked corn bread,* he thought. *My favorite.*

Clara's father, Owen Gills, slid a wooden paddle underneath a

cast-iron pan and pulled it from the oven. He set the pan of golden-brown corn bread on the counter and rested the paddle against the wall.

"Good morning, Lucas!" he said. "What brings you to the bakery so early?"

Lucas rubbed his stomach. "Well, I *always* come for your baked goods!" he said. "But I also came for Clara. We have some official business to attend to—a request from my father, King Caleb."

Mr. Gills served a piece of corn bread to the prince.

"Clara will be pleased to hear it," said Mr. Gills. "I expect her back any moment. She's finishing her chores."

No sooner had Mr. Gills said this

than the back door unlatched and swung open.

"Here I am!" sang Clara. "And you're right, Father, my chores are all done!" She turned to Lucas with a big smile. "So what's the big news?"

Lucas swallowed a mouthful of food. "All is not well in Bogburp," he said. "And there's urgent royal business we need to attend to!"

Clara's face lit up. She *loved* royal business. It meant one thing—adventure! She grabbed a square of corn bread and took a big bite.

BOGBURP

WARNING!
BOGS, ALLIGATORS,
SNAKES, STENCH,
AND WITCHES!

"What's the problem?" she asked, leaning in.

Lucas quickly wiped the crumbs from his mouth. Then he took a deep breath. "As you know, it's been storming all across the kingdom for days," he said. "The strange weather patterns seem to be coming from Bogburp, and Grom suspects Tilda the witch is up to something."

Clara's eyes grew wide. "I had a feeling there was something weird going on!"

Lucas lifted his hood and covered his head. "Me too!" he agreed. "Grom asked the king if we could investigate."

WELCOME TO
BOGBURP
HOME OF THE MARSH WITCHES
HAVE A LOVELY STAY

Clara eagerly turned to her father, who had been listening.

"You have my permission," Mr. Gills said with a nod. "But you two be careful. Anything that involves witchcraft is dangerous."

Clara grabbed her cloak and then gave her father a big hug. "Don't worry. We promise to be safe."

"Yes, that's a double promise!"
Lucas added. Then the two best
friends hurried out the door.

Lucas unhitched Ivan and gave
Clara a ride to the royal stables to
pick up her own horse, Scallop. Dark
clouds raced overhead, and thunder
rumbled in the distance.

Clara held tightly to Lucas, eyes straight ahead. It didn't matter what was waiting for them in Bogburp. Whatever it was, an epic adventure was about to begin.

CHAPTER 2

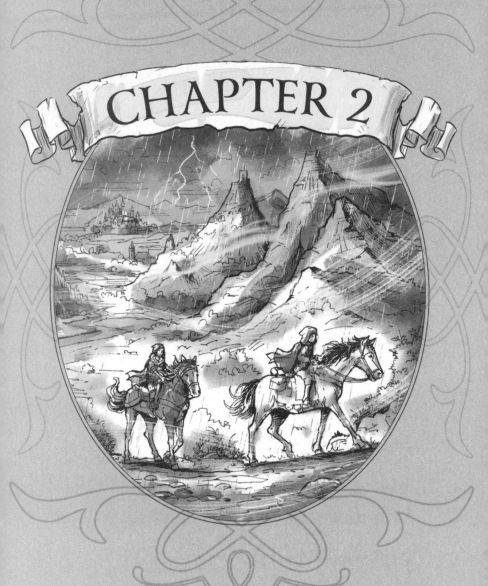

Knock! Knock!
Who's There?

Scallop munched a bundle of hay while Clara quickly secured her saddle.

Then Lucas and Clara bounded toward the swamps of Bogburp. The strong wind and rain spattered their faces as they rode up the mountains.

Their first order of business was to find Tilda the witch.

Like many of the witches' homes in Bogburp, Tilda's was built in the branches of a gnarled old tree with a thick trunk. An uneven boardwalk spiraled up the trunk to a wooden door.

The kids tied their horses to a log rail. The boards creaked underfoot as they walked to the front door. Clara lifted the bronze pine cone door knocker.

Thunk! Thunk! Thunk!

They listened for footsteps. But nobody came.

After a few seconds Prince Lucas tried. Still no one answered. So the kids walked around and peeked into the windows.

"I don't think she's home," Lucas said.

But that's when they heard a noise coming from higher up.

Tap! Tap! Tap! The kids craned their necks.

"I don't see anything," Clara said, confused.

"Neither do I," said Lucas. "Let's climb higher."

So the kids walked around the boardwalk, circling the tree. They stopped and tilted their heads back again.

"Hey! I see someone!" said Lucas, pointing to the upper branches. Clara followed the prince's gaze. And there, on the boardwalk farther up, stood a girl in a purple hat. In her hand she held a twisted stick with a glowing amber sphere at the end.

"Look! She has a wand," Clara whispered. "She's not Tilda, but I think she's a witch."

They leaned down and watched the young witch. She lifted her wand and pointed it at a bouquet of pink flowers. With a magical chant and a flick of her wrist, the flowers turned from pink to blue.

"Oh, shigglety shoots!" the witch
complained. She waved her wand
again. This time the flowers turned
from blue to red.

"You're supposed to turn *yellow*,"
she said, scolding the flowers.

As they watched a handful of nonharmful spells continue to go wrong, the kids decided it was safe to step in. So Lucas stood up and cleared his throat.

"A-hem! A-HEM!"

The witch jumped and pointed her wand at both of them. "Hey! Who's out there?" she cried.

"Oh, please don't be alarmed," Lucas said carefully. "I am Prince Lucas of Wrenly, here with my friend Lady Clara. We mean no harm!"

CHAPTER 3

Head Games

The young witch lowered her wand and lost hold of it.

She bowed down as it clattered onto the deck.

"Oh, Your Highness!" she cried, picking up her wand. "I'm sorry I pointed my wand at you. My name is Clover."

Lucas and Clara walked up the boardwalk to greet Clover properly.

"It's nice to meet you, Clover," said Lucas. "We didn't mean to startle you."

Clover shook her head, blushing.

"You seem a bit frustrated," Clara said. "What is it you're trying to do?"

The witch looked at her wand and shrugged her shoulders. "I'm *trying* my best to be a good witch-in-training," Clover said. "Tilda's been giving me lessons, and I was practicing for an important spell exam." She paused and let out a big sigh. "I'm supposed to make these flowers turn yellow, but I can't seem to get it right."

Lucas and Clara looked at each other, not sure of what to say. They both took potions lessons at the castle, but they didn't know much about wand magic.

The young witch tapped her foot nervously. Then she stopped as her face lit up.

"Hey, I know!" she said, lifting her wand again. "My spell book didn't say this magic worked on flowers. But I know it works on *hair*!" Clover leaned over eagerly. "Do you want to see? On hair it's totally foolproof, I swear!"

Clover was sure she'd finally be able to do something right. So before the kids could say a word, she aimed her wand and chanted:

"Flippity flop!
Bippity bop!
Swap your hair color!
Swippity SWAP!"

Lucas and Clara covered their heads and shut their eyes tight. *Poof!* A cloud of magical dust wrapped around them. They bent down as it swirled faster and faster.

Clara began to cough as swarms of dust lifted up. And Lucas was starting to feel dizzy.

Until finally the chaos stopped.

Clover watched and waited for the magical dust to clear. But when the kids stood up, Clover let out a panicked gasp.

The kids then looked at each other in horror.

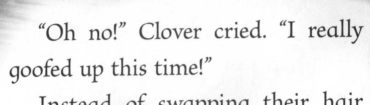

"Oh no!" Clover cried. "I really goofed up this time!"

Instead of swapping their hair colors, Clover had swapped Lucas's and Clara's entire heads!

CHAPTER 4

The Book of Counterspells

Clara pointed to her own face and head on Lucas's body and shrieked.

"Lucas, something is terribly wrong!" she cried. "You have my face and head!"

The prince covered his mouth and pointed back at Clara. "Well, *you* have *my* head!" he yelled in a total panic.

In that moment lightning cracked and thunder rumbled, as if the sky knew something dangerous was brewing.

The two friends whirled around and glared at Clover.

"What have you done to us?" Lucas cried.

Clover didn't dare look them in the eye. Her wand shook in her hand.

"Oh, zookers!" she said. "I can't believe I botched another spell! I must be the kingdom of Wrenly's worst witch."

Tears started welling up in her eyes.

Prince Lucas suddenly felt bad. "You put us in big trouble," he said firmly, "but you're the only one who can help us."

"Yes, of course," Clover said, wiping away a tear. "Please come inside the tree house. There must be a counterspell we can find."

Clara didn't love the idea of trusting Clover with another spell. But she knew Lucas was right.

While Clover unlocked the door, Clara quietly tapped Lucas on the shoulder—or rather, *her own* shoulder.

"Did you notice all the lightning and thunder after Clover performed the spell?" she whispered.

Lucas nodded without looking at his face on Clara's body. It was too weird.

"I did," he replied. "This wacky weather seems to have something to do with Clover's faulty spells."

A few moments later Clover led them into the tree house. The inside of the house had a very witchy look. Tilda had a wand collection, crystals, a cauldron, a dragon chess set, broomsticks, pumpkins by the fireplace, and a library full of spell books.

The young witch scurried over to the shelves. As she pulled a bunch of books out, she flung one at Clara by accident.

"Ow!"

The Book of Counterspells

"So sorry!" Clover said, dragging a chair over so she could climb up and see the books on top. She tapped the spine of each book with one finger as she read more titles. Finally she stopped on a leather-bound book with gold writing.

"This is the one we need! *The Book of Counterspells!*" Clover cried. "I have to admit, though—I've never performed a counterspell before."

Lucas and Clara looked at each other nervously.

"Clover, you're the only one who can fix us," Prince Lucas said. "You have to focus and *believe* in your magic."

Clover nodded firmly.

No matter what, this time she had to get the spell right.

CHAPTER 5

Switchity! Swappity!

After reading through almost every spell, they finally found it.

"Hmm," Clover said as she read the book. "'Have you lost your head?! Perhaps you've swapped heads with somebody else—or with something else? If you're feeling out of your head, then this spell will return your head—face, brain, and hair—to its proper location.'"

Ingredients

1 pickleweed plant

FIG.1

1 rainbow leaf

FIG2

DRY!

FIG3

1 piece of dry oak wood

1 bucket of oak sap

FIG 4

FIG 5

1 mandrake root

FIG 6

1 rabbit's foot

FIG 7

1 barrel of swamp water

Heat the swamp water in your cauldron and add all the ingredients. Stir until the mixture boils. Then chant the following spell:

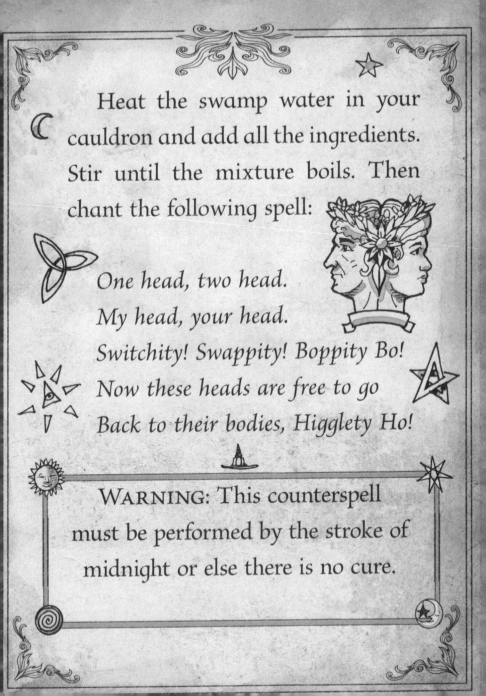

One head, two head.
My head, your head.
Switchity! Swappity! Boppity Bo!
Now these heads are free to go
Back to their bodies, Higglety Ho!

WARNING: This counterspell must be performed by the stroke of midnight or else there is no cure.

Lucas peered out the window to see where the sun was.

"It's already midafternoon?!" he said. "We'll have to work fast to beat the stroke of midnight! Clover, do you have these ingredients?"

Clover studied the list again.
"No, but I know where to find them.
We'll need to split up. Prince Lucas,
you'll go to Ravenna's Apothecary
to get mandrake root and a rabbit's
foot."

Lucas nodded as he took note of his task.

Then Clover turned to Clara and said, "You'll be able to find rainbow leaf at Margrove Lagoon. And I'll go to Ash Pond for the pickleweed."

"What about the oak sap, oak wood, and swamp water?" asked Lucas.

The witch pointed toward the window. "We are surrounded by those, so we can get them last."

She drew a map to the apothecary for Lucas and a map to Margrove Lagoon for Clara. Then the two friends quickly changed into each other's clothes. On the outside, you would never know anything was wrong.

Now that they had a plan, Clover grabbed her broom. "We'll meet back here at sundown," she said. "Good luck to you both!"

The kids waved as the witch whizzed out the door.

"Well, I guess we'd better *head* out too," said Lucas with a chuckle. "Get it? *Head* out."

Clara tried to keep a serious face. But even she had to admit, this was turning out to be one of their strangest adventures yet.

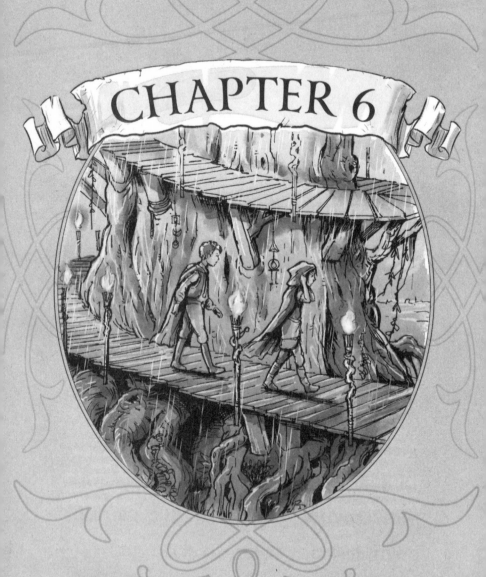

CHAPTER 6

Ravenna the Witch

The kids hurried down the board-walk, back toward their horses. Lucas now had Clara's face and was wearing her clothes. And at least on the outside, Clara was now the prince of Wrenly.

Lucas had never imagined what it might be like to switch places with his best friend. It was strange, but kind of fun at the same time.

Soon the kids unhitched their horses. But since they were both in disguise, their horses wouldn't move on command. So they had no choice but to switch horses too.

"I have to head west," said Lucas. "There's a compass in the pocket of my tunic if you get lost."

"Well, I'm going east," Clara said. "And my pocket holds a stopwatch should you need it." Then she slapped her reins. "See you at sundown, and good luck!"

"Same to you!" said the prince. Then he rode off in the other direction.

Lucas arrived at Ravenna's Apothecary on the edge of Bogburp. The apothecary was a large round hut made of upright sticks, mud, and a thatched roof. Scraggly, twisted vines crept up the sides.

Lucas shook a rope with bells right beside the door.

Jing-a-ling-a-ling!

A witch with dark black hair, green eyes, and a pointed black hat opened the door.

"Hello, are you Ravenna?" asked Lucas.

The witch didn't so much as smile at the prince. She simply raised one eyebrow. Bogburp rarely had human visitors, let alone kid visitors.

"Ye-e-e-e-s-s-s," she said, meowing the word "yes" like a cat. She looked Lucas up and down. "And what brings the likes of *you* to Bogburp? Have you lost your way, child?"

Lucas stepped back in surprise. Everyone usually knew who he was. But that's when he remembered that right now he was Clara.

"Yes, if I may, I'd like to come in," said the prince, glancing in the window. "It doesn't look very busy inside."

Ravenna drew in a deep breath and opened the door a bit wider. Lucas stepped into the shop, which was also Ravenna's home.

The showroom was like being in a witch's candy shop. Shelves and tables were stocked with crystals, seashells, fish bones, potions, herbs, dried flowers, charms, beads, and a

wide selection of broomsticks, wands, and cauldrons.

The prince wandered around, taking a close look at everything. Ravenna dusted trinkets as she kept one eye on her customer. Finally Lucas spied a basket with rabbits' feet. He picked a tawny-colored one.

Against one wall stood barrels of plants, herbs, and roots. He grabbed a fistful of mandrake root from a bin. After one last look around, he set the items on the counter.

"And how do you plan to pay for this?" Ravenna asked quizzically. Lucas didn't have any money, but he did know how to make a deal.

"I can grant you a favor from the prince whenever you need it," he said. "I know him and give you my word."

Ravenna's eyes lit up. A favor from a prince could come in handy. "And how am I supposed to trust your word?"

Lucas pulled out Clara's royal stopwatch, which had the crest of the kingdom of Wrenly. Ravenna knew that a commoner would not own something of such value without palace connections.

73

Then the prince wrote a note of promise, signed it, and held out the watch.

"Take this watch," he said. "And if you come to the castle, give this note to a palace guard."

The witch grabbed the two things. Then she put the rabbit's foot and mandrake root in a bag.

"You may go this time. But I will hold you to this promise," she said.

Lucas nodded, took the bag, and slipped out into the rain. The storm had gotten worse, and night was coming quickly.

CHAPTER 7

See You Later, Alligator!

Clara galloped along a forest trail, holding her map in one hand. The wind whipped her hair this way and that . . . until a strong gust blew the map from her hand!

Clara—who was not used to being in Lucas's boots—hopped down from Lucas's horse. She reached over and carefully plucked the wet map from the swamp.

"Oh no! The ink smeared, and now I can't read it!"

Clara looked around, not sure what to do. And that's when she spied big, big trouble. Two alligators were crawling out of the swamp, and their snouts were pointed right in her direction.

Ivan, who was usually a very brave horse, whinnied and ran for safety. So Clara sprinted toward a nearby tree too. The alligators picked up speed—jaws open. Clara shimmied up the trunk, grabbed a branch, and pulled herself up.

She climbed to a higher branch, panting to catch her breath. She stared down at the alligators. They hissed. Clara shuddered at the sight of their jagged teeth.

Oh no! I'm stuck in a tree and trapped by alligators! she thought. *I have to stay calm and scare them away.*

So she snapped a branch and shook it at the alligators. But they didn't budge. Clara groaned. She needed another plan, but she had no ideas.

Then she heard a familiar squawk.

She looked at the sky and saw Ruskin, the prince's pet scarlet dragon.

"Ruskin! Down here!" Clara cried. Ruskin swooped down and blew a stream of fire at the alligators. Then he chased the alligators back into the swamp. He flew to Clara and helped her down.

On the ground, Ruskin circled her and sniffed her. Of course, she smelled like Lucas. But the dragon could sense that something wasn't right.

"Ruskin, you can trust me. It's me, Clara," she said, patting his head.

"Lucas and I are in trouble, and we need your help."

With that, Ruskin squawked loudly. He was always ready to help his friends. So Clara slid onto the dragon's back.

Together, they looked for Ivan and found him hiding in a grove of trees. Clara hopped off the dragon and onto Lucas's horse.

"Ruskin, we need to find Margrove Lagoon," said Clara. "Do you know where that is?"

The dragon bobbed his head and took flight.

Nobody knew the kingdom of Wrenly better than Ruskin. Clara knew she could trust her brave friend and followed the scarlet dragon to a beautiful hidden lake.

Ruskin flew down and circled a large patch of rainbow leaf. Rainbow leaf grew in the water, but Clara couldn't go swimming in Lucas's royal robes. So Ruskin flew back and carefully carried Clara to the middle of the lake.

As the dragon dipped low over the water, Clara tugged on a big clump of rainbow leaf. The rainbow leaf stems snapped, but as she pulled back, Clara lost her balance.

"Who-o-o-a-a!" she cried, slipping off Ruskin's back. But the dragon quickly wrapped his tail around her before she splashed into the lake.

"Wow, thanks, Ruskin! That was close!" she said. "Now take me back to Lucas's horse, Ivan, and let's ride. We haven't much time at all!"

CHAPTER 8

The Great Oak
Comes Alive

Clara spied Lucas and her horse, Scallop, approaching Tilda's tree house from the opposite direction.

"Lucas!" cried Clara.

The prince waved as Ruskin flew to his best friend.

"What are you doing here, boy?" Lucas said. The dragon happily nuzzled against the real prince. "I'm so glad to see you."

"Did you find your ingredients?" asked Clara.

"Yes, I got everything on my list," he said. "How about you?"

Clara nodded. "Me too. We'd better get inside. It's getting dark."

So Lucas and Clara tied their horses to the log rail, and Ruskin

stayed outside. The kids shivered as they ran up the boardwalk. Their clothes were wet from the rain.

"Oh, good—you're back!" said Clover, waving the kids over to the cauldron. The house smelled like boiling swamp water. "Did you find everything?"

Lucas and Clara held up their ingredients. Clover sighed with relief. The wet rainbow leaf dripped on the floor.

"Quick, we need to add everything to the cauldron," Clover said.

One by one, Lucas and Clara dropped the ingredients into the pot. The mixture bubbled wildly.

"Now all we need is a piece of oak wood and its sweet sap," said Clover, stirring the mix. "Let's collect it together." Lucas and Clara pulled up their damp hoods and followed Clover outside.

The witch stood at the base of the tree and pointed her wand at the trunk. Then she chanted this spell:

"Tappity! Tap! Tap!
On the old oak tree.
Sappity! Sap! Sap!
Come to me!
Stickety! Wickety! Whee!"

Sparks flew from Clover's wand. She held out a bucket for the sap. But instead of the tree releasing its special sap, its branches moved and came to life.

"Uh-oh!" cried Clover as the kids backed away.

The branches, like long bark-covered arms, reached down and wrapped around Lucas and Clara. Then the branches lifted them into the air, swirling the kids around.

"HELP!" they both cried.

Ruskin heard the kids' cries and flew to them right away. The dragon fought to free them, but the powerful branches pushed the mighty dragon away. Lucas and Clara were now prisoners of a magical old tree.

CHAPTER 9

The Magic Ingredient

Clover dropped her wand and covered her face with her hands.

"I'm the *worst* witch in the world!" she cried. Ruskin flew to her side and gave a roar of warning. With that, Clover snapped back to attention.

This was no time for a pity party! She needed to release the kids and reverse the spell before they were all in *worse* trouble.

Clover covered her ears so she could think. Then she remembered that Tilda had cast a protection spell on her property to protect her magical secrets. If the oak tree sensed it was being attacked, the spell would kick in.

I know the counterspell, Clover thought. *I've heard Tilda recite it before.* Clover quieted her thoughts as best she could. Then she chanted the spell:

"Oh, magic oak tree, fear no harm. Let this spell break your charm."

Zap! The tree stopped thrashing and let go of Lucas and Clara. Ruskin swooped in and broke their fall.

"I did it!" Clover cried as the kids scrambled to their feet.

"Well done, Clover!" the prince said. "Now let's get back to the cauldron before we run out of time!"

Everyone raced back into Tilda's tree house, including Ruskin.

Lucas and Clara studied the spell book to make sure Clover hadn't missed anything. That's when they found a possible error.

"Clover, a lot of these spells you've been practicing call for *dry* oak wood. Since it's been raining, the oak wood is wet. This may be what's causing all the problems with your spells—including this nonstop rain!"

Clover checked the spell and saw that they were right.

"And there's one more thing you must do," Lucas added.

Clover raised her eyebrows. "What's that, Prince Lucas?"

The prince smiled. "You must believe in your own magic. My father, the king, taught me to have confidence in everything I do—even when I don't feel it. Confidence is the magical ingredient to anything."

Clover nodded thoughtfully. "I do mumble most of my spells—that's because I'm afraid they won't work."

But with the support of her two new friends, she was ready. She took a deep breath and marched outside.

This time, she returned with a smile and a bucket full of oak sap.

"Well done!" said Clara. "Now all we have to do is dry the oak wood."

So Clover bent down and set the wet oak wood near the fire. Right as she turned back to the cauldron, Tilda's old clock struck eleven-thirty.

They only had thirty minutes left to undo the spell and turn things back to normal.

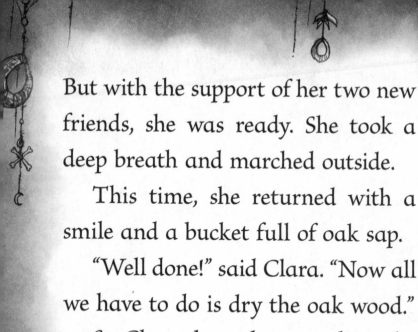

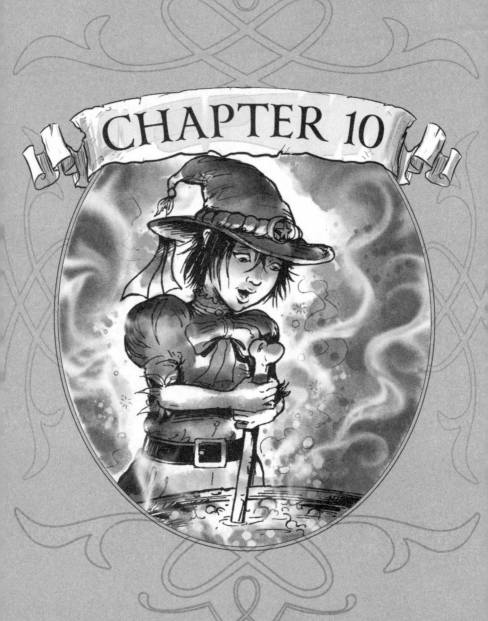

CHAPTER 10

Bubbles and More Troubles

The kids watched Clover drizzle the oak sap into the brew. The cauldron boiled furiously. She stirred the pot and chanted the spell:

"One head, two head.
My head, your head.
Switchity! Swappity! Bippity Bo!
Now these heads are free to go
To their bodies, Higglety Ho!"

Poof! A cloud of magical dust burst from the cauldron. When the dust cleared, Clover poured the potion into two cups. She held out one for Lucas and one for Clara. But that's when Ruskin got a tickle in his nose. . . .

ACHOOOOOOOO!

Ruskin sneezed and knocked the potion from Clover's hands. *Poof!* A cloud of magical dust whooshed into the air. When the cloud cleared, Clara's head was back on her shoulders! But now there was a new problem.

This time the prince's head was on Ruskin's body and Ruskin's head was on the prince's body! Lucas began to walk on all fours while Ruskin squawked in panic.

"Oh dear! Clara cried, looking over at the clock. "We have to make another batch of potion, and fast!"

There were less than five minutes until the stroke of midnight.

So Clover quickly poured more swamp water into the cauldron and added the ingredients. She stirred the brew and waited for it to boil. When it bubbled, she chanted the spell. Then she ladled the potion into a bowl for Ruskin and into a cup for the prince.

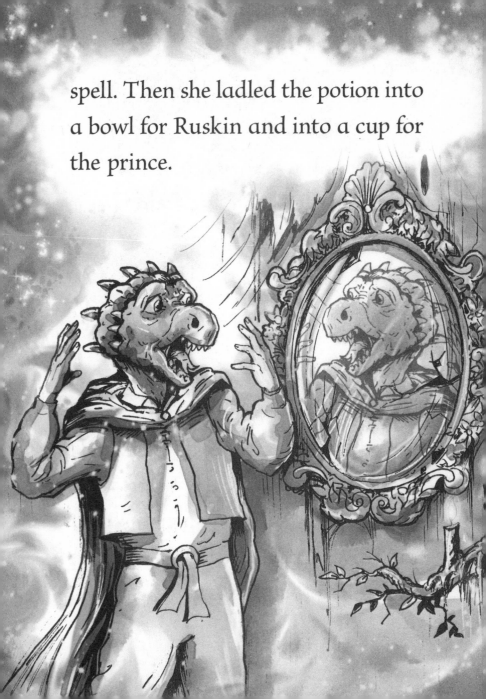

"Drink up!" she cried. Lucas
chugged the potion, and Ruskin
lapped his from the bowl. *POOF!*
Magical dust covered Lucas and
Ruskin once again. When the dust
settled, the prince and the dragon
looked like themselves.

"You did it!" cried Lucas, grinning from ear to ear.

"Sorry about that," Clover said sheepishly. "And thanks for all your help."

Ruskin squawked loudly as the clock finally struck midnight and the front door swung open. It was Tilda the witch!

"My goodness!" she cried, setting down her broom. "Why didn't I get an invitation to this royal midnight party?"

The kids looked at one another and burst into laughter.

"Welcome back, Tilda!" said Clover. "You're right on time for a celebration!"

So Clover heated biscuits and cider, and everyone sat down beside the warm fire. Then Clover and the kids took turns telling Tilda about their crazy adventurous day.

"And after all that, guess what?" asked the prince, looking out at the full moon. "The rain has stopped, and our mission is *almost* done!"

Their last order of business was for Ruskin to send news back to the castle. The kids would return with their horses as soon as the sun rose.

It had been a long, strange, and stormy day. But thanks to Prince Lucas and his friends, all was well and back to normal in the kingdom of Wrenly—right at the stroke of midnight.